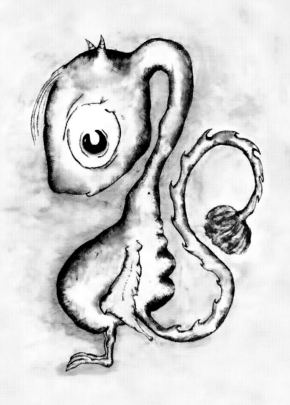

The Lonely Little Monster

a Worrywoo tale

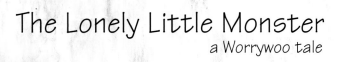

by Andi Green

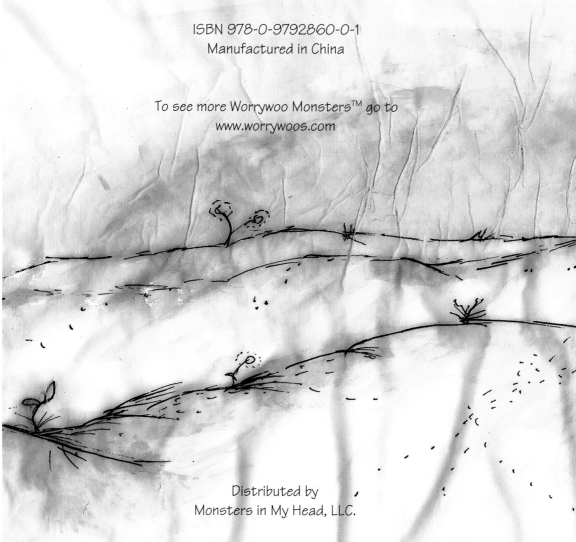

ISBN 978-0-9792860-0-1
Manufactured in China

To see more Worrywoo Monsters™ go to
www.worrywoos.com

Distributed by
Monsters in My Head, LLC.

This book is for my mom.
Thanks for never giving up on me.

Once upon a time,
in a far away land

lonely little Nola

sat in the sand.

Counting her fingers
and counting her toes

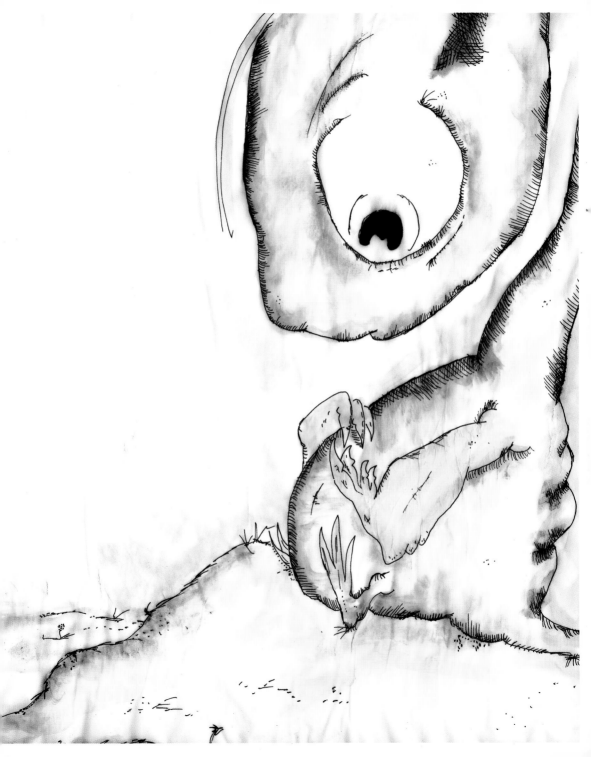

wishing for love
     and someone to know.

"Anyone

there?"

she would ask the big Sky.

But, all she would hear

e?

Anyone there?

Anyone there?

...was her echo reply.

Anyone there?

Anyone there?

The minutes became hours

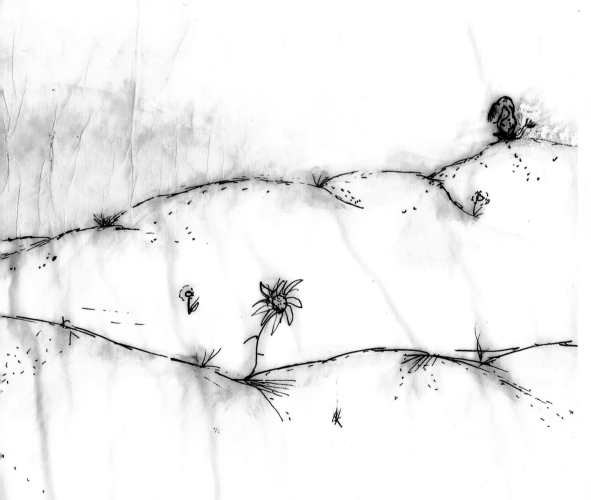

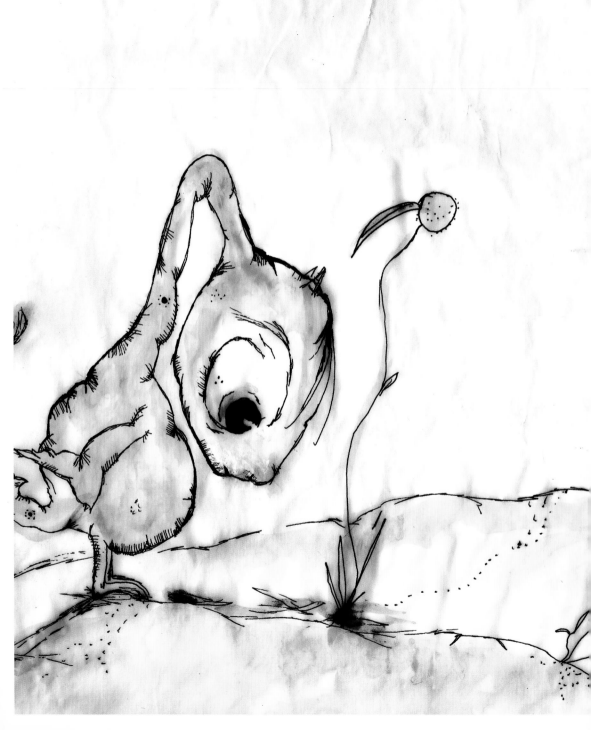

which turned into days

as she begged the bright Sun

"Will you please stay?"

But, the Sun never answered
and
always
went
down

leaving her quietly with
no one around.

To sweet little Nola,
        no friend was in sight

so she cried fifty days
   and sighed forty nights.

And her loneliness

lingered,

feeling harder to bear

until she awoke

to strange

Sounds

in the air.

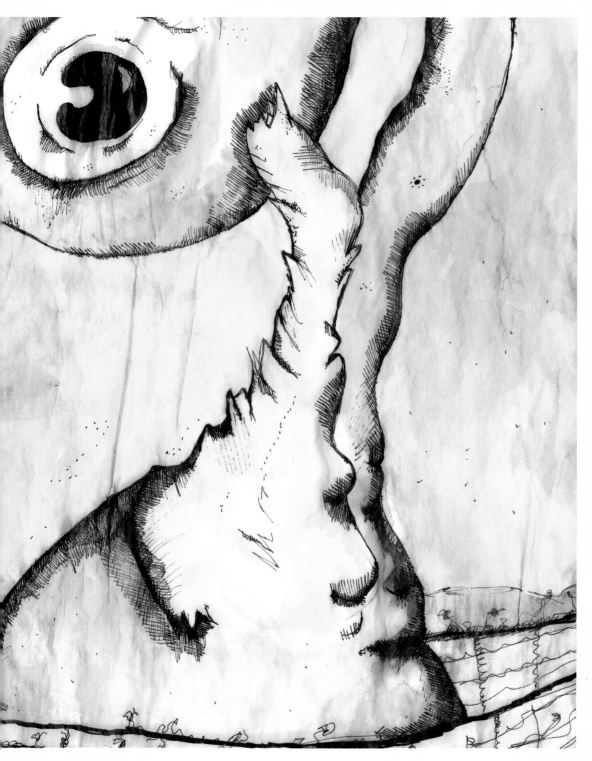

Of waves that were

Cras

hing

and seemed to appear

like an

ocean

of feelings brought out by her tears.

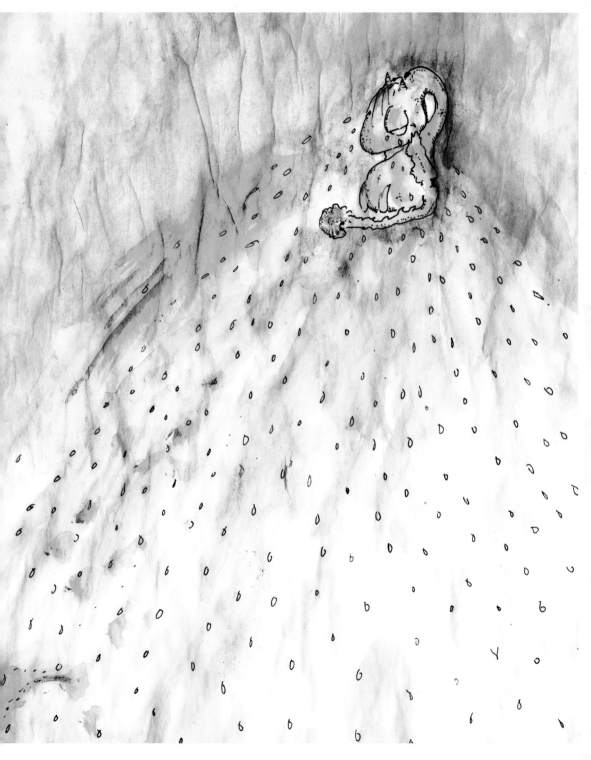

As she ran to get closer

she

stopped...

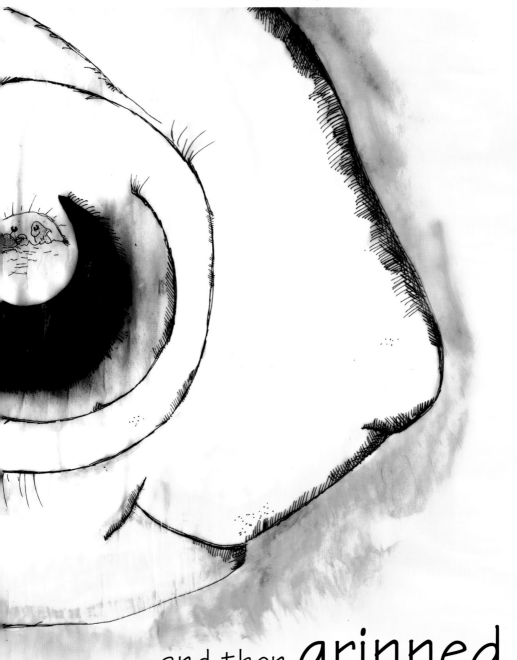

and then grinned

at all the new

creatures with

pincers

and fins!

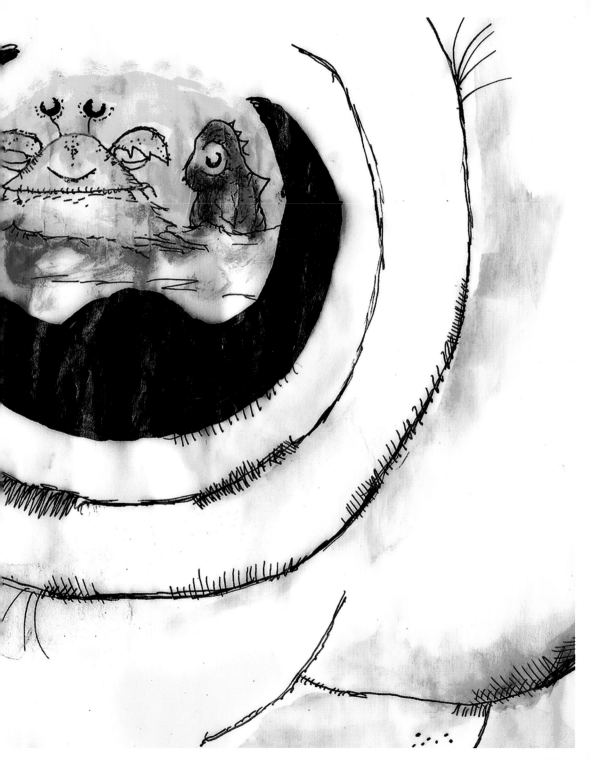

"WHERE HAVE YOU BEEN?"

she shouted with glee.

"We've always been here

you *just didn't see."*

So, if you feel lonely cause
no one's in sight

look outside of

yourself

and maybe you might

see others
like you who
want to
be found-

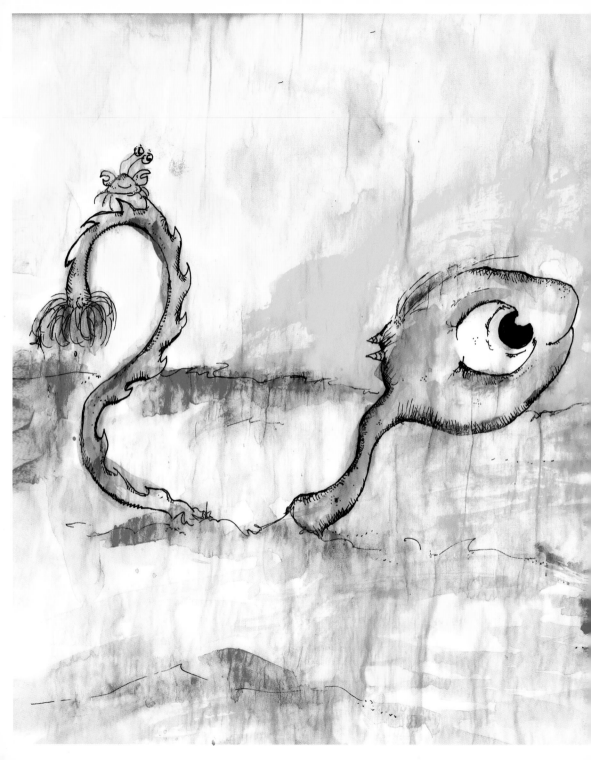

Give it a try ... just look around!